GRANDMA'S SILENT AUCTION
February

BY: MICHAEL JAMES

Copyright © 2020 by MICHAEL JAMES

All rights reserved.

No part of this book may be reproduced in any form or by any electronic or mechanical means, including information storage and retrieval systems, without written permission from the author, except for the use of brief quotations in a book review.

CHAPTER ONE
CIARA

I have been home for a full day. My heart is in a million pieces. My brain is messed up. I am so confused and lost. I have cried and when it stops, I cry some more. I hate this. I don't want to continue with my Grandma's stupid auction. I want to close my eyes and open them to realize this was just a dream. No, that isn't true. I want to open them and be back with Malcolm. I want to wake in his bed, eat dinner with him and when the day ends, go to bed with him next to me. I want to be with Malcolm. He makes me happy. I feel loved and cherished when we are together. What the ever loving fuck was my Grams thinking? Was I not supposed to have a strong connection with any of these men? I mean seriously, she set me up with ten men. How did she not think my heart wouldn't get broken? I don't think I can do this. This hurts. I am not daring enough to keep an open mind. I'm scared that in the end, I am not going to come out of this as a whole person. Up until now, I thought I was doing just fine. I have my business. I had a boyfriend. Mostly, I had a heart that wasn't broken.

I throw my blankets over my face. I am not getting dressed or anything else today. I don't care that Grams wants to see me. I am not going to her stupid mansion. She can forget it. She might be lucky if I even talk to her ever again. Maybe I should return the favor and auction her off like a beef cow. Show her how much this whole plan of hers sucks. I would love to see her drown herself in a bucket of tears. Leave her heart in another state while going off to meet some other guy across the country. She would see for herself that it isn't so easy.

"Go away," I yell when my doorbell chimes. This girl isn't home.

It chimes again. Ugh! I am not answering the door.

"Ciara, open this door."

I leap from the couch and run to open the door. I open it, pulling Porter inside, then hurry to shut and lock the door. I then throw myself into his spread arms. I don't care that his arms have bags hanging off of them.

"Whoa! Did you miss me?"

"You have no idea!" I break. The tears start flowing like a waterfall down my cheeks.

"Oh, dear, what happened?" I can't even answer him. He wraps an arm around me and the bag that is on his arm hits me in the butt. *"Let me put these bags down then we will sort you out."*

"There's no sorting me out. I'm a wreck and it's all Gram's fault."

I move out of his arms and run back to the couch. I grab the blanket and throw it over my body, covering my face. I can hear Porter putting stuff in the refrigerator. I hear dishes rattle. What the hell is he doing? I peek. Oh, ice cream! I sit up and wipe my eyes. I have the bestest friend. He really is wonderful and knows me so well. He hands me a bowl of mint chocolate chip. I take it, not wasting a second to drown out my sadness in ice cream.

"Okay, spill. What has you puffy and red-eyed with hair all over the place?"

"Malcolm Miller. Porter, he's amazing."

"Then why the hell are you crying?"

"I love him."

"That's nothing to cry over. You should be shouting from the mountain tops or some shit like that."

"Are you listening to me? Don't you see the problem here?"

"No, I don't. Unless he isn't in love with you, then I could see why the waterworks are flowing."

I slap his arm. "He does love me back. The problem is he sent me away anyway. 'If we are meant to be together, nine months shouldn't stand a chance.' Blah blah, bullshit."

"He's right you know. A lot of couples spend months apart and they survive."

"Yeah well, they don't date nine other men in between."

"Typically not. He knows the rules and situation. It's what he signed up for. Did he say he'd wait for you?"

"Yes, but."

He cuts me off. "No but's, Ciara. If he said he'll wait for you and you trust your relationship is real, then you have to wait it out."

"Whose side are you on?"

"Yours, always yours."

"It doesn't sound like it."

"I want the best possible guy out there for you. This is one hell of a way to find him. Now tell me all about Malcolm."

"He is so handsome, intelligent and so romantic. I swear he can read my mind."

"And he looks like?"

"He's not as tall as my norm, but still taller than I am. He has dark hair, brown eyes and a beard that he keeps trimmed. He doesn't like to dress up and he doesn't make his employees dress up, either. Porter, he is nothing like Hunter at all."

"Phew, that's a relief."

"His family is just as cool as he is. You'd get along with all of them. He's very protective of his younger sister."

"Sounds like a great guy. So, no more tears. If he's this amazing guy, and you two are destined to be together you will be."

"Why are you frowning?"

"Don't take this the wrong way, okay?"

"Okay!"

"Hunter was and is a douchebag. Malcolm probably is this great guy that treated you the way a lady should be treated. I think you should continue this journey your Grams put you on."

"Why?"

"Because you should make sure he wasn't a rebound guy."

Now, I frown. Malcolm isn't a rebound guy, is he?

I did not throw myself at the first guy who was nice and respectful to me, did I? What if Porter is right? Nah, he is way off base with this one. *"I guess it will make the next man on Grams' auction list the next rebound guy."* Just saying that out loud is wrong.

"I did not say that. But now that you have, it's pretty much true." I put the bowl on the end table. Now, I'm getting pissed off. *"Listen, you need to get it in your head that this is an adventure to find love. You are going to laugh, cry, have great sex and do so many different things. Be open-minded, turn your heart off and when the time comes to make a choice, listen to your heart then."*

"Turn my heart off. You make it sound so easy."

"It's not going to be, but it's how you will get through this."

"Hell, Porter, I'm on the first guy. Next year, I'm having Grams auction you off and then you'll see how difficult this is."

"Please do. My love life is stale." Porter leans over and gives me a hug. *"Now spill the juicy shit. Is he a dud in bed or he knows how to get you off?"*

"I am not sharing my sex life with you."

"You're no fun!"

I smile. *"A girl doesn't kiss and tell. However, I had many orgasms."*

"Sign me up for next year!" We laugh. *"I need to get back to work. Claudia was left alone."*

"What's in the bags?"

"An order. Since you are banned from coming to work, I brought you a distraction."

"Oh, I like."

"Everything you need is there. I'll swing by tonight and get it."

"Okay."

He stands and leans over to give me a hug. *"Get out of that head of yours. See you tonight."*

"Love you, Porter!"

"Love you, too, Ciara."

Turn my heart off. That is horrible advice. I wouldn't know how to do that even if it were possible. It's too late to do that anyway. I already left it on for Malcolm. I can't change that nor do I want to.

I look at the bags Porter left on the breakfast bar. Perfect, I need this. It's the best way to get my mind off everything. I get up from the couch. I rub my hands together. I hope it's a gown or something that will occupy me for the rest of the day.

CHAPTER TWO
CIARA

I leaped off the couch and ran to the door, still half asleep. I never made it to my bed last night. I parked my ass there after Porter swung by to pick up the dress I made for a special request. I regret opening the door once I get my bearings. Stupid me was dreaming and when the knock woke me, I didn't check the peephole. I whipped that door open, ready to jump into Malcolm's arms. Instead I was staring my Grams in the eyes. Well not really in the eyes since she has on her oversized sunglasses still. I could tell right away she wasn't happy with me. I have avoided her ever since I've been home. Guess what Grams, I'm not too happy with you either!

She pushes her way into my place. Her driver must be new. I haven't ever seen her before. *"Who are you?"*

"Patty Fox, but you can call me Pat."

I roll my eyes. I'm already irritated. *"Grams, where is Beckett?"*

"He's downstairs waiting for me."

I snap my head back at this new lady. *"Who are you again?"*

"Patty, but you can…"

I cut her off. *"Yeah, I can call you Pat. I got that part."*

"Ciara, stop being a brat to your new driver."

I push her out of my doorstep. *"Excuse us for a moment."* I shut the door. *"What the hell is going on?"*

She whips her sunglasses off. *"Well, my sweet Granddaughter, Pat is here to drive you to Florida since you missed your flight."*

"I'm not going anywhere. I'm done with your little adventure as you like to call it. You know, Grams, it feels more like a game. A game with my heart. I don't care to play."

"No matter what you want to call it, it's for your own good." She moves my blanket and sits down on the edge of the seat cushion. *"Sit down, Ciara."* She pats the spot next to her. I don't move from my place. *"Now,"* she demands. I huff. I am very irritated. *"You know, I never found that right person to share my life with. I drowned out everything to do with love to*

focus on making my designs and a name for myself. One day, I thought for the first time in my life I would meet a guy who would stand by me, love me and all that good jazz. I was wrong. I had your mother and raised her alone because I didn't find that perfect guy. Sadly, your mother fell into my footsteps when it came to finding a good man. I won't let that happen to you."

"I understand you wanting the best for me. I really do. But having me date hand-picked men from you isn't the way it should work. Malcolm is an amazing guy who I fell in love with. I don't want to meet these other men."

"You did just hear what you said to me, right? I hand-picked him for you and look at what happened. For you to know your life's journey should be with a particular man, you have to go through the ups and downs together. You being separated from Malcolm for nine months isn't just a test of your love and devotion to him, but of his to you as well. If you are meant to be with him, your path will lead you right back to him. Nothing beats love that can handle whatever is thrown onto your path."

"This is interfering with letting nature take its course."

"No, it's not. Have you thought about the fact

that, yes Malcolm may be this wonderful man that you fell for right off the bat. That first initial spark dwindles after the first few months of a new relationship. One of these other nine guys may outshine Malcolm or that spark is going to light a fire inside you and it's going to burn and burn inside your heart."

"I don't get how you survived all these years alone. You sound like a hopeless romantic."

"I wish I hadn't spent all these years alone, Ciara. I look back at all the lonely times in my life and I have regrets. I just can't let you make the same mistakes."

"It bothers me to know that you don't think I can do this on my own."

"Sweetheart, it has nothing to do with whether or not you can do this on your own. I just know how ambitious you are and you will neglect finding love. Before you know it you're my age and all alone."

"You honestly think if he's the one we will end up together at the end of this? Grams, I fell hard and quick for Malcolm."

"In nine months you'll have the answer. Not all these men are cut out to be with my fashionista girl."

"So what now?"

"Now you are going to get that little hiney of yours in the shower then get in a car with Pat who will take you to Hawk Evans."

"Who is he?"

"The love of your life or a speed bump in the road." I roll my eyes. *"Is it safe to let your driver in now?"*

"Yes. I better get in the shower."

"Love you, my girl. I'll see you in March."

"Grams, why am I not allowed to call you at all?"

"Never said you couldn't. I just figured you didn't need me."

"So, I'm allowed to call you and Porter?"

"Yep. No work, young lady."

She gives me a kiss on my cheek then puts her sunglasses on. I roll my eyes, for a woman who eats and breathes fashion, she has no clue they look horrible on her. Maybe I should find her the perfect pair.

My Grandma lets Pat back into my place on her way out. I know I owe this lady an apology. I was being a brat as Grams said. She stands at my door not moving an inch. Is she even breathing? I walk over to where she stands.

"Hi, Pat. I'm Ciara Verbank." She shakes my hand. *"I'm sorry for my rudeness. I hope you can forgive me."*

"I think we can put it past us and move forward."

"Good, come on in and make yourself at home. I just need to shower and then I'm all yours."

"Perfect."

"There's bottled water, soda or orange juice in the refrigerator if you are thirsty. I shouldn't be too long."

"Good, because we are running a bit behind schedule."

I nod. I am still wary of my Grams idea on this journey of love, but I do know, I want a man to spend the rest of my life with. Maybe this is the right direction and I will find what I want at the end of this madness. I really hope I don't fall in love with them all. If I do, what will I do, flip a coin and hope for the best?

I never thought I'd have a personal driver of my own. I have been chauffeured around when I am with Grams, but having my own, oh no. I could very well afford one, but I like to drive. Plus it's not like I go to very many places anyway.

I tap on the window divider and Pat puts it down. *"Can I help you?"* I don't answer her. Instead, I climb over to the front seat. Pat is surprised by my actions. *"Something wrong?"*

"Lonely back there and this is going to be a long trip." The expression on her face is priceless. *"So, tell me where are we headed?"*

"Florida."

"What part of Florida?"

"Daytona."

"Did my Grandma hire you today or have you worked for her before?"

"I don't work for your Grandma, Ma'am. I work for Mr. Evans."

Oh, that's surprising. This might be an educational trip. *"What's he do for a living?"*

"I'm allowed to chit chat with you as long as it's not about Mr. Evans."

"Why?"

"I don't know. When I got pulled from the airport to drive you, it's what I was told."

"By Him?"

"No, by your Grandma and his personal assistant, Bethany. Mr. Evans acted like he didn't know what the hell was going on."

"Is he from here or does he live in Florida?"

"Neither one, Ma'am."

"You can call me Ciara, you know."

"Thank you."

Talking about my next boyfriend is out of the question, I guess we will make small talk for the next twenty hours. Now I kind of wish I didn't miss my flight to Florida. This is going to be one hell of a long drive. I reach back into the backseat and get Alaska. I hug and kiss her. Too bad Pat wasn't driving me across the country instead. I really miss Malcolm.

CHAPTER THREE
CIARA

This trip has been one hell of a long drive. I catnapped a few times and each time I fell asleep my puppy woke me up. She decided to sleep only if I were awake. Pat and I had to stop more than she would have liked for potty breaks. That led her to put the pedal to the metal and scare the ever-living shit out of me a few times. It didn't matter how many times she told me she was trained for this kind of driving, it still scared me. Christ, a few times she was weaving in and out of traffic like she was being chased by someone. I thought I was going to piss my pants. I wanted to tell her I think Mr. Evans would like me alive after spending a shit ton of money on me to be his girlfriend for the next month. About the only thing I thought was cool about the trip was how this sweet woman can drive like a maniac. I wondered if she tells her church ladies how crazy she drives. Oh and the palm trees. I like those as well.

"We are almost there. I gotta say, we made up some lost time. You might be a little early if we get through this traffic without hitting every light."

Please hit every light! *"Where are you taking me?"*

"To the hotel where you'll be staying."

"Oh." I guess I won't be staying with Mr. Evans as I did with Malcolm. That might be better. That way I can have my space and just maybe stay out of his bed.

Not even five minutes later, we pull into the hotel. Pat pulls up in front of the immaculate hotel. At least from the outside, it is. I get out. Wow, it's much warmer here than at home. I tell Pat I'm taking Alaska for a walk. She told me she'll get me checked in and wait for me in the lobby.

I put my pup down on the sidewalk. She starts to walk off. It's been a while since we last stopped. We round the corner and take a path to a very small grassy area. It's more like dead grass. I can see the ocean and the air is salty. I see only one other person out here with me. He has a dog as well. I try to go in a different direction but Alaska has a mind of her own.

We get to the person walking his dog. His dog smells mine and my puppy thinks the bigger dog wants to play.

"Careful, my boy might eat your tiny little thing for lunch."

Well hello to you too, grump ass! *"He doesn't seem like he wants to eat my puppy."*

"What kind of dog is that anyway?"

"A Pomsky. Yours is a Husky, right?"

"Husky-wolf mix."

"Oh! He's beautiful. Alaska is part husky."

"I know what a Pomsky is. I meant why on earth did someone mix a great breed with such an annoying barking twat."

"Oh, wow!" That comment catches me off guard. He called my dog a twat! I look around in shock. *"Well, have a good day."* I pick up Alaska and walk away. What the hell was that about? Rude asshole. I mean, holy fuck, he is a jerk. He didn't need to insult my poor puppy. I have half the mind to turn around and tell him off. You know what, I'm going to do just that. *"Hey, just because you think your dog-wolf doggy is better than mine doesn't give you the right to be a prick."*

"Whatever!"

"Are you always a dick? Good God, you remind me of my ex-boyfriend."

"Have a good day."

I stand here dumbfounded. If this is how people are in Florida, I want to go home. And they say New Yorker's are unpleasant.m!

I start to head back to the hotel. Pat probably thinks I got lost. At this point, I wish I could. I make sure I stay far enough back that I don't have to talk to the asshole again.

My puppy barks. *"Don't pay any attention to him. He's just an asshole with a big chip on his shoulder."* Alaska barks again and the jerk looks back at us, with a smirk on his face. What does he know? My puppy rarely barks.

I get inside and watch the man and his beastly dog go to the elevators. Great, he's staying here. I sure hope we don't meet up again.

"There you are. Thought I was going to have to send out a search party for you."

"Nope, not lost. Still here." I smile a fake smile.

"Here's your room key card. You are on the second floor. I'll be waiting right here for you in one hour."

"What happens in an hour?"

"I will take you to your next destination." Oh, good I can hardly wait. *"Go freshen up!"* She shoos me away with the wave of her hands. Christ, I'm going. I could use some alone time, anyway.

I get up to my room and check the room out. It has a nice view of the ocean. There is a balcony, a kitchenette and a large bathroom with a stand up shower and bathtub. The king-size bed looks cozy. I guess this room is alright. It's not home, though.

I look in the stuff that I packed. I didn't get as much information about Hawk Evans from Pat as I'd hoped for. I have to admit I didn't read the tidbit of information that my Grams offered to share with me. Unfortunately, I didn't read it, nor did I bring the binder with me. I am going to meet this man without knowing anything about him. It is not like I knew much about Malcolm when I met him, so this shouldn't be much different.

Pat is driving me to meet Mr. Evans. She told me I had to sit in the backseat. I tried one more time to get her to spill the beans on him, but she remained tight-lipped. All she said was she wished she could partake in our date. She can gladly take my place and I don't even know what we are doing.

I get the first glimpse when she turns into a parking lot. All I can think is, what in the world are we doing here! I sure as hell hope I'm not getting into one of those go-karts. I seriously hope this guy is the owner or some shit like that.

Pat lets me out. I see a man waiting at the entrance. I close my eyes as he smiles at me. He's a tall guy with salt and pepper hair. He has a mustache but no beard. He comes toward me and when he's in front of me he says my name. I think my tongue is tied. I'm very nervous, so I just smile and nod my head.

"I hope your travels were well."

"They were, thanks."

"I hope you are ready for a race!"

"Umm, not really. I've never been in one of those before." I point to the go-kart.

"Well, let's get you in one so that I can teach you how to run one. First, we need to get you in a helmet." Oh lovely, just what I want to do; not. *"The place is closed just for us. So no need to worry about other karts getting in your way."* Well, that's a little relief.

I get a helmet on. I am so glad I wore jeans, a

light sweater, and tennis shoes. I can't picture myself in a go-kart in a dress and heels. Hell, I can't picture myself in one of these death traps no matter what I am wearing. No wonder Ms. Hot Rod Pat wanted to be on this date!

I get in my car and Mr. Evans goes over all the ins and outs of the mini wannabe car. I double-check my seatbelt. *"Hang tight. When you see the flag person, wait until she drops it before taking off."*

"Okay. Can I go slow?"

"Ya, if you want to lose the race, sure."

I narrow my eyes at him as he walks away. I don't like him already. He's short with his words, he didn't introduce himself, and he never even asked if I wanted to do this. When the flag drops, I might not even move. Ha, take that, Mr. Evans.

Shit! The flag girl is standing at her post. I glance over at the car pulling up next to me. He revs his engine. Damn it, now I have to race him. He takes off. Shit! I hit the gas pedal and spin the tires. I hit a tire or two as I round the first curb. This isn't so bad. I can do this. I get bumped from behind. What the hell? How in the world did he get behind me? He whips past me. That's when I realize how slow I'm going.

We do ten laps. Okay, he does ten laps and I do five. We get told to pull off to the side. I do and get my seatbelt off and get out. The guy in front of me takes his helmet off. Fuck, you've got to be kidding me. I want a rematch, I shout without thinking. He narrows his eyes at me and puts his helmet back on. I see the guy I met at the gate. He shrugs his shoulders. Jerk!

CHAPTER FOUR
HAWK

I have had a really shit day. It first started out with a long conference with the higher-ups. I find long meetings boring and I see no reason why I had to sit through it. It had nothing to do with me personally whatsoever. It's something that my manager or boss should have handled. I could see me having to be there if it were promotional or whatever. Once I got out of the three-hour conference, I had to board a plane that isn't mine. I had to fly first class instead of taking my private plane because it had something wrong with it. I don't even know what the problem was. Bethany just handed me a ticket and put me in a cab to the airport. On top of all that, where the hell was Pat?

By the time I reached Florida, I was not in the best of moods. I checked into a hotel ready to just relax and unwind with a nice dinner and turn in early.

Tomorrow is such an important day. Then I get told I must be somewhere I don't want to go. Hell, I didn't even know what the place was. However, when I arrived, my mood changed slightly as soon as I saw four wheels, a steering wheel, and an engine. My manager stood at the stand with a helmet in his hand. Fantastic, I get to whoop his ass in a race. I put that helmet on, climbed into the go-kart and I was ready. My mood instantly got better. I bumped him a few times as he drove like a turtle around the track. I am not ashamed I passed him five times. I was livid when I found out that my manager wasn't in the other go-kart. I had no idea that was a girl I was bumping into. I never would have acted that way. Whatever my manager is up to, we will get to the bottom of it as soon as I beat this girl at another race.

I park my go-kart and get out. *"What the fuck was that? I thought it was you and I racing. Who the hell is that girl?"*

"Calm down, Hawk."

"Calm down? Are you serious right now? I could have wrecked her." I see her out of the corner of my eye taking her helmet off. I turn my head to get a good look at her. You've got to be fucking kidding me! *"You're the dog girl."* I throw my hands up in the air. This day couldn't end any faster.

"Where are you going?"

"To the hotel."

"Take Ciara with you."

I turn around and keep walking backwards. *"Why would I do that?"* I turn back around.

"Because you'll be with her for the next month."

I stop in my place. I repeat his words in my head. I spin on my heels. *"What?"* I walk back toward them in a hurry. This girl is trying really hard not to look at me. I have my hands on my lower waist. I want answers.

"How about I give you two privacy."

My manager doesn't allow her to leave. *"Ciara Verbank, I'd like you to meet Hawk Evans. Hawk, this is Ciara."* She doesn't extend her hand and neither do I. *"Hawk, Ciara will be traveling with you for the next month."*

Like hell she is! *"What for?"*

"She's your girlfriend for the month."

"Ciara, I'm going to have my driver come pick you up and take you back to the hotel. I need to have a talk with my manager."

"Okay," she quietly says.

I watch her walk away and when she is out of earshot I look at my manager in the eyes. *"What the* hell is wrong with you? I have no goddamn desire to date and you know that!"

"Listen to me very carefully, Hawk. I have your best interest at heart as always. I know you don't want a girlfriend, but having one is good for your image. No one says you have to sleep with her and do the whole love thing. Just take her on dates and be seen with her where the media can get all warm and fuzzy inside."

"Let me get this straight. You hired me an escort for a month for you to pull off this publicity stunt?"

"She's not an escort. She is a very well-known clothing designer. Women all over the world wear her clothes and boy are they going to be jealous of her being on your arm."

"Why would a woman of such renown agree to be a fake girlfriend?"

"The girl's Grandma auctioned her off. Guess Grandma is looking for love for her Granddaughter."

"And she agreed to it?"

"Must be. She's here isn't she!"

"You people are all fucked up! I'm going back to the hotel. Leave me alone for the rest of the day."

"So, you'll do it?"

"I didn't say that! See you tomorrow."

Seriously, what the hell is wrong with these people? You can't play with people's emotions this way. It's wrong on so many levels. Carl should know me well enough to know that I don't play games. I am who I am regardless of what the others are doing to shape their images. Like me or hate me, I stay true to myself.

I wait for my ride at the gate. I had Pat take the girl back to the hotel. I send her another text telling her to come and get me, now. Just as I pocket my phone, she whips into the parking lot. I laugh. Pat is very well trained in how to drive. I think she loves the hustle and bustle of traffic.

I get in my car. *"Where to, Mr. Evans?"*

"The hotel please."

"You got it."

"Did you get the girl there without problems?"

"The girl," she chuckles. *"Ciara was dropped off safely."* Ahha, that's her name. I need to remember that. *"She's a lovely girl."*

She got that out of a five-minute drive? *"I bet she is."*

"You know I drove her here from New York?"

"You did what!?"

"She missed her flight. I think on purpose. So, Bethany and her Grandma had me drive her."

Now it makes sense why I had to take the hotel's

shuttle service from the airport. And Bethany knew about this and didn't tell me? She's going to get an earful later. First, I need to know what Pat knows.

"What makes you think Ciara might have missed her flight on purpose?"

"She wasn't happy when I showed up with her Grandma at her place. She told me on the drive how her Grams auctioned her off behind her back."

Hmm, this is good information. The poor girl is in the same boat as I am. I wonder what made her show up. Maybe I'm a publicity stunt to her as she is to me. This might not be too bad of an idea as long as she and I are on the same page. It could be a win win for all involved.

I tell Pat I won't be needing her anymore tonight and that she should get some rest. Before I exit the car, I also tell her to be ready at seven in the morning.

CHAPTER FIVE
CIARA

After the long drive and meeting Mr. Attitude I came back to the hotel, showered and crawled into bed. I am so mentally drained that I really need a good night's rest. If I have any luck at all, Hawk sends me home. I cross my fingers he does just that. He doesn't seem like he's very happy with his life. I don't think he knew anything about me being here at all. He seems just as blinded by all this as I was.

I am just about asleep when my puppy licked my face. I peek one eye open and I hear her whimper and I know I had better take her out. I'm quite pissed that I have no clothes to wear besides the ones I wore. From now on, I'm bringing clothes with me. I am thrilled that there's at least a hotel bathrobe I can put on over my bra and panties. It's not the way I'd like to dress going outside of the room, but I guess it'll have to do.

I get outdoors and set Alaska down. She really must have had to go because she wasted no time doing her business. I am relieved as I am tired and just want to get some rest. As I am walking back through the lobby, I see a gift shop and it gives me an idea. I then see business cards and go over to grab one. I am going to need the address. I hear a commotion behind me, coming from the hotel's lounge. I hurry and make myself scarce when I spot Hawk sitting at the end of the bar, staring right at me. I have sleep to get and I don't need his attitude right now.

I get back to my room and crawl up onto the bed. I use my phone to find a shopping or strip mall nearby. I see one of the stores nearby carries the MV brand. I feel like I hit the jackpot. I call the number listed for the store. I wait until she does her greeting before I speak.

"You sell the MV line of clothing, correct?"

"Yes, ma'am we do. Can I help you find something you are looking for?"

"You might be able to help me find a lot of stuff. Are you the owner or manager?"

"Sorry, I'm just a sales associate."

"I am Ciara Verbank, I am the designer of the MV clothes. I am in desperate need of clothes. The airline lost my luggage." I lie a little.

"Oh, that stinks. We are open until nine tonight if you'd like to come in."

"I was hoping we could do a little phone shopping and delivery. I'll totally pay you to be my personal shopper."

"You can shop on the website."

"I'll tell you what, if you help me right now, I'll buy you whatever you wish from my website and I'll pay you tonight for your troubles."

"Okay, but how am I supposed to know what you'd like?"

"Got a cell phone?"

After forty-five minutes of FaceTime with the girl, I have a new wardrobe on its way after she closes the store. It wasn't too bad of an experience. I have to say the girl was quite knowledgeable about everything that was on the racks of mine. I have to make sure I pay her well and get her information so that she gets what she wants off my website.

Now, I just have to stay awake long enough for her to get here then I can sleep.

Fantastic, I managed to stay awake long enough to get my clothes, crawl back into bed, and I've been tossing and turning the last hour. You ever get so overtired that you can't sleep? That's me right now. I can't find dreamland and it's irritating me. Which isn't helping me at all.

I sit up in bed and startle Alaska. At least one of us can sleep. She let out a sigh to let me know I disturbed her then went right back to sleep. I get out of bed. I have to find something to wear me out enough so I can get some rest. I could go for a walk, but then there's a chance of running into Hawk. That's the last thing I want to do. His attitude will only frustrate me more.

As I pace the room, I remember seeing a sign for an indoor pool. I fiddle through the clothes and find the bathing suit I picked out over the phone. I smile. I like swimming and I hope it will relax me to the point of not being able to keep my eyes open. I study myself in the mirror. Gosh, it's more revealing than I thought. I grab the bathrobe and slip it on over my suit and get a towel. I cross my fingers I'll be the only one in there.

I make my way down to the first level and follow the sign. I am glad the lobby is quiet and seems deserted. Maybe luck will be on my side and I'll have the pool to myself. When I reach the room it's dark. There aren't any lights on besides the lights inside the water. I check the hours and it doesn't say it's closed, so who needs a lot of lighting.

I pull the door open and a blast of warm air hits me. The smell of chlorine fills my nose. It probably would have been smart of me to have wet my hair first, but the hell with it.

I find a lounge chair and set my towel down. I take the robe off, setting it next to the towel. My hair is in a messy bun, so I take it down and run my fingers through it. I walk over and dip my toes in the water. It's actually quite warm. Warmer than I thought it would be. I walk down to the deep end. It brings back a childhood memory of when I was terrified of diving in. The kids picked on me, calling me chicken. That only encouraged me to do it. I was so proud of myself for overcoming a fear. My teacher was so impressed by my dive and the distance I went before needing air, he asked me to join the diving team for swimming. I was on the team for a year before I quit. Fashion meant more to me and I felt diving took too much time away.

I dive into the water. The rush and the blast of water feels so good against my skin. I come up for air and swim the rest of the way to the shallow end. I get out and do it all over again. When I reach the shallow end this time, I decide to float around and relax. I had not realized how much I miss being in the water before now.

I feel calmer and more relaxed. Probably enough to sleep. I get out and when I'm heading in the direction of the lounge chair, I can't resist diving one more time. I go to the deep end and I hear a noise. I look around and don't see anything. Maybe it was just the heat or something turning on. It could have been someone out in the hall. I shrug a shoulder and dive in, there's nothing to make me feel scared. This will be my last swim before I go back to my room. I sure hope this worked.

CHAPTER SIX
HAWK

I was sitting in the hotel's lounge having a drink when I saw Ciara in the lobby. I was sitting there drinking my soda and contemplating whether or not I could go along with this scheme my manager has cooked up. I still feel it's the wrong thing to do. I see how it could backfire on everyone. My name already has this bad boy image attached to it and if it gets out that the relationship is fake, it could make me look worse. I was reaching for my phone to text my manager to tell him I was not doing this when I saw Ciara. I paused what I was doing and watched her. She had her puppy in her arms. Her bare leg peeking out of her robe as she glided about. She stopped at the front desk and took something and then disappeared. I glanced back at my phone, picked it up and put it in my pocket. Maybe I'll wait until tomorrow to make up my mind.

I paid my tab and as I was walking out of the lounge, I felt hands on my arm. I turned my head to the side and a couple of girls were all star struck. What I want to do is yank my arm away and continue on to my room, alone.

"*Ladies,*" I say.

"*I told my friend you are Hawk Evans and she doesn't believe me.*"

I smile. I could totally fuck with them, but I don't. "*Yep, the one and only.*"

"*Oh, my God. I knew it.*"

"*She has a huge crush on you. Can we get a selfie?*"

"*Sure, but then I have to go. I have a very busy day tomorrow.*" The girls cozy up to me and I hold the one's phone out in front of me and snap a picture. I feel a hand copping a feel of my ass. I smile and look at my fan. "*How about we do one with just the two of us?*"

"*I would love that.*" I put my arm around her shoulder and smiled for the photo. I snapped the picture and gave her the phone back. The one who grabbed my ass thought she'd get one as well. I step away and blow a kiss to my fan. "*Have a good night.*" I know ladies well enough to know that burned the second girl's ass. I guess she should not have touched mine.

I don't go to my room. I should try and get some sleep but I'm not ready for that. I walk past the elevator and take the hallway that I have no idea where it leads to. That is when I find the gym. Perfect, just what I need to burn off some energy. I go back toward the elevator and go up to my room to change. I haven't worked out in a couple of days. With my career it's important to stay in shape.

I get back to the gym and I am glad that I'm basically alone. One guy notices me and I think he recognizes who I am, but he leaves me be. That is a rare thing. Usually, they always strike up a conversation or want a photo. I get on the treadmill to warm up after I do a few stretches. I set the speed to a jog to start out. I generally jog for about a half hour. I scan the weight room and I am quite pleased this gym has everything I tend to use. I can work my entire core muscles. I want to do my arms, but with it being such a big day, I don't really need sore biceps tomorrow.

I worked out for a little over an hour. When I leave the gym I spot the pool room. The lights are bright and I see a few people lounging around. I am such a dick at times, but hey, why not use my status once in a while to benefit me. I go out to the front desk. I ask for the evening manager. I tell him I'd like the pool to myself. He glances at his watch and tells me the pool closes in five minutes.

"Do you know who I am?"

He gives me a funny look. *"I'm sorry, sir, I do not."*

"I am Hawk Evans." He stares at me as if I have two heads. *"Google me."*

He gets out his phone and does just that. *"Let me see what I can do."* I nod. I wait for him while he goes into the office. When he returns he says, *"It would be against safety rules if I lock the door, so I won't be able to let you have the pool to yourself. The lifeguard is off when it closes."*

"How about this, you clear it out, don't lock the door and dim the lights to make it appear closed." I would slip him a hundred if I had my wallet on me. Money talks I've learned in this life of fame.

"Fine by me. Don't be drowning in there."

"I'm a good swimmer," I joke.

Ten minutes later, I have the pool to myself. I sit in a dark corner, taking my sneakers off. I notice someone entering. Not just someone, it's my fake girlfriend. I sit back and watch her. Holy hell that swimsuit she wears gives me a good look at her body. I'd be lying if I said she isn't hot. She definitely has my attention.

I watch her as she dips her toes in the water before going to the deep end. It's dark enough that I almost lost her, but then when she stands above the water ready to dive in, the lighting from the pool's lights brings her back into view. She dives in and it's a smooth dive. I lean forward watching for her to pop up. When she does, she swims to the shallow end to where I am. I lean back so that I stay hidden in the dark. I watch her get out and do it all over again.

I sit here and pondered whether or not I should show myself. She might think I'm a perv hiding in the dark. Although, I was here first. She intruded on my private time. Didn't she think the lights were off for a reason?

She gets out and I think she's going to leave. She changed her mind and went back to the deep end. I stand and the chair scratched on the cement flooring. I know she heard it, but she blew it off. She dives in and I get out of the shadows and get in the pool. She didn't see me when she came up from the bottom. She swims to the end to get out, but before she does, she dunks her head back into the water to get her hair off her face. I surprised her by swimming to where she is. I laugh when she screams.

"What the hell! You shouldn't do that to a person." Ciara moves past me to get out.

"Are you leaving?"

"Does it look like I'm leaving?"

"Yes."

"I guess that's your answer."

"You are a great diver."

"How long have you been in here?"

"I'd say maybe a minute or two before you came in."

"You've been watching me? I didn't see you."

"I was sitting over there." I use my head to show her.

"In the dark like a perv."

"Hey, I was here first. I was taking my shoes off when you intruded on me."

"Well, now you can have the pool to yourself."

I wrap an arm around her waist, stopping her from getting out. *"What if I want you to stay?"*

"I'm tired."

"C'mon, stay for a little longer."

"Why would I want to do that? You've been a..."

I don't know what comes over me when I silence her with my mouth. I kiss her with dominance. She's stiff at first and her hands are on my shoulders trying to push me away. I am about to stop and let her go when she relaxes and her hands wrap around my neck. I pull her closer to me. Then I grab her ass, lifting her. Her legs wrapped around my waist. She throws her head back and I kiss the front of her neck, tasting the chlorine. She lifts her head when I take my lips away.

"Who are you, Ciara Verbank?"

"I should probably go."

"I don't want you to go."

"I got a different impression this afternoon."

"I'm sorry for what I said about your dog. I know it's no excuse, but I was having a bad day. I also had no idea I was racing you today. I thought you were my manager."

"I accept your apology."

"So, you'll stay and swim with me?"

Her eyes search mine. She smiles. *"I will, on one condition."*

I smile, too. *"What is that?"*

"We dive. If I dive further than you, I go to bed. If you beat me, I'll stay."

"I don't know if that's fair, but I accept because I like the challenge."

Her legs fall from my body. She splashes water in my face and laughs. She laughs and it echoes. I grab her again and toss her over my shoulder. Damn, her ass feels good under my palm. I dunk us under. She gasps before we hit. We come back up.

"That is not fair."

"You'll learn this month how much I don't play fair." Did I just confirm that I'm doing this dating thing for a month?

Ciara pushes my shoulder and takes off. She gets out of the pool and says, *"Are you coming or are you chickening out?"*

One thing I am not is a chicken. I get out and catch up with her. I grab her and throw us both into the pool before we reach the end. She squeals mid-air. We come up and she wipes her hair from her face. We tread water. She laughs and tells me I'll pay for that. She tries to splash me again, but I catch her arm. I drag her over to me. I place a hand on the back of her neck and kiss her again. This pool air must be dogging my brain. Suddenly, I want this woman. I want to rip the bathing suit off her and fuck her right here.

CHAPTER SEVEN
CIARA

I stretch out my back and yawn. I definitely didn't get enough sleep last night. I throw the blankets off my lap and look around for Alaska. I call out her name and find her chewing on my shoe. No, damn it. Those cost me a small fortune. I pick her up and tell her she's a bad puppy. She licks my face. I may have to kennel her at night. This is the second pair she has chewed.

I walk over to the door with her in my arms. *"I wonder if that's Hawk. Don't worry he's sorry for basically calling you a twat."*

I open the door to a lady. *"Good morning, Ciara. I'm Bethany, Hawk's personal assistant."*

"Hello, what can I do for you?"

"I am supposed to take you shopping."

"I did that on my own."

"Sorry about that. We will reimburse you for that expense."

"I got it covered."

"Not the rules. I'll just need your receipts."

I roll my eyes. Stupid rule if you ask me. *"Is there anything else I can help you with?"*

"Well, how about breakfast?"

"Umm, sure. Will Hawk be joining us?"

"No, he left an hour ago. It'll be just the three of us."

"Three?"

"You and the pup."

"Oh!" I smile. This is a bit awkward. *"I need to get ready if we are going to breakfast."*

"Okay. Want me to take the pup outdoors while you get ready?"

"Umm, sure. Her name is Alaska."

She takes my baby. *"I'll send someone up to pack up your belongings."*

"Why?"

"We'll be leaving after breakfast."

"Where are we going?"

She gives me a look as if I'm clueless. I am and I know I'm coming off that way, as well. *"Have you met Hawk, yet?"*

"Yes. We did a go-kart race where he thought I was his manager. The meet didn't go so hot." I don't tell her about the pool because I feel it's none of her business.

"What do you know about him?"

"That he can be an ass. Sorta good-looking. Oh, and that he has a dog."

She just stands here staring at me. *"Hmm,"* she finally says, *"how about you get ready and we can meet in the lobby. I'll fill you in a little about my boss."* She looks at her phone. *"Half an hour good with you?"*

"You know, I don't have a suitcase. My clothes are still in the bags, so I don't need someone to pack for me. I can be ready in a half hour."

"Good, does this little thing have a leash?"

"Yeah, let me get it for you." There's something about her that I don't really like. She seems like a snotty bitch. I wonder what Hawk does for a living that he needs an assistant. I give her the leash. She hooks it to my baby's collar. *"I'll be down soon."* She begins to walk away. *"Oh, hey, is there a certain way I should dress?"*

"Jeans and a shirt will be fine." Jeans and a shirt when she's dressed in a pencil skirt. I stick my tongue out at her behind her back. Bethany is

nothing like Malcolm's lady. Denise is so much nicer.

I get in the shower. Mentioning Malcolm's name makes me miss him. Now, I'm feeling guilty about the pool last night. After Hawk threw us in the pool, he kissed me again. He didn't break the kiss until my back hit the side of the pool. I held on the side to keep my head above water. He held on one-handed. His other hand crested my body. His knuckle ran over my erect nipples. He untied the strap from behind my neck. My top floated away. I leaned my head back and closed my eyes as he cupped my breasts. My legs pulled him closer and I felt his cock was hard between us. Hawk pulled the strings on my bottoms, getting them out of the way. I told myself I should stop him and just go to my room. Then he kissed the front of my neck all the way to my ear. He whispered in my ear with his stern voice that he wanted to make me cum. In my head, I wanted to tell him no. However my body was saying something entirely different. I lifted my legs higher. Then I felt his hand grab my ass then slide downward, toward my pussy. His fingers teased my lower lips. All while having his body pressed into mine. I moaned when he worked his fingers inside me. I gripped the pool's edge tighter when he moved his fingers around inside me. It felt good. I turned my mind off and let my body go. I wanted him to give me an orgasm. Let go, he told me. I did and he swam us to the shallow end to where the steps are. I sat on the top one. My body out of the water beside my feet. Hawk continued with fucking my pussy with his fingers. I was on the verge of an orgasm when he stopped. He then leaned over my body, telling me he wants to fuck me. I nodded my head. He flipped me over. He got behind me and slid his cock inside me. He pounded his shaft in and out of me with his hand on my throat. I loved every second of how rough he was being. I reached between my legs and played with my clit until I orgasmed. He wasn't far behind. He pulled out of me and stroked his cock until his cum marked my back and ass. I couldn't believe this man that was insulting earlier gave me an orgasm in a public pool. Thinking about how dirty that was turned me on. I could have gone for round two, but I got out of the pool instead. Hawk got out as well. His manhood was still hard. I looked away before I attacked him. I hurried and got my robe on.

I shake my head and turn the shower off. What the hell is wrong with me? I have feelings for Malcolm and here I am turning into a slut. What does this say about me? I hate that I am beginning to question the feelings that I know are real. There has seriously got to be something wrong with me to cheat on such an amazing guy. I can't mess that up. I need to learn to keep my legs closed for the next nine months.

I met Bethany in the lobby and we went to breakfast. She didn't tell me anything about Hawk at all. I sure did get her life's story though, right up to the point of her starting to work for my boyfriend. I was annoyed that she kept going on and on about herself and never once asked about me. Every time I would try and get information about Hawk she seemed irritated. Something is going on here. Either she's trying really hard to not tell me what Hawk does for a living or she is just narcissistic. Heck, maybe she is secretly in love with her boss and is trying hard to tell me nothing about him. It could be she doesn't want me to get close to him at all. I wondered how she would act if she knew he already had sex with me.

Pat drove us to breakfast and is now taking us to wherever Hawk is. I watch out the window so that I don't have to look at Bethany. I have no desire to talk with her anymore. Instead of sitting next to her, I wish I could climb up front with Pat.

"I let Carl know we are here. He'll meet us at the trailer."

"Who is Carl?"

"Hawk's manager. I thought you said you met him yesterday?"

"I did but he never told me his name."

She sounds frustrated when she says, *"That man is hard to deal with."*

I stop myself from laughing out loud. I think they are all hard to deal with. No wonder Hawk is grumpy. He hangs around assholes. Besides Pat, I like her. She's very sweet. Even when she drives crazy.

"We are here." I snap out of my thoughts. Where the hell is here? All I see are what looks like tour buses.

"Pat, make sure you get all of Ciara's bags inside the bus."

"Will do, Ms. Bethany."

My car door is opened by Hawk's manager that I now know is Carl. He holds out a hand for me to take. Not that I need his help, but I put mine in his. He tells me he will take me to Hawk and that we need to hurry before we miss him. He informed me that we are a little late. I yell over my shoulder to Pat and thank her.

I look around and I am piecing together who Hawk Evans is. At least I think I know. Carl hands me a badge and tells me to put it around my neck. I do. I read it as I walk fast to keep up with Carl. We reach an area and Carl shows me where to sit. He gives me headphones and I put them on. A car whips by us so fast, I barely saw it. I look at the screen in front of us.

"Is Hawk driving that car?"

"Yes. He's going super fast."

Wow! He's a race car driver? That's cool, but holy shit! I know nothing about racing besides cars go fast around a track in a circle. This is exciting, I guess.

Carl elbows me. *"If he goes this speed later, he'll probably get the pole."* He points to the screen. Holy shit! They go that fast? *"That a boy, Hawk. Can you save the speed for later? I don't need you tearing up the car before practice."*

"Ah, chill out, old man, I got this. This car is sweet."

The car stops right in front of us. Hawk turns the car off, puts the black net down on the window and puts the shield up on his helmet. He gives Carl a thumbs up. He looks right at me and winks. I smile. I am suddenly feeling giddy inside. I'm dating a racer for the next month. This could be exciting. He climbs out of the car, takes his helmet off and comes to where I am. Carl plays a video for him of his laps. His excitement is like fireworks going off. I like this guy much better than the one I first met.

CHAPTER EIGHT
HAWK

Getting in my car this morning is just what I needed. After having the last two months off it's like a rebirth. Racing is my life. There is nothing in this world that excites me more than my car. The butterflies that fill a driver's insides are driven on pure adrenaline. It's the rush of a lifetime each and every time the engine fires up. Driving a car that goes 160 to 200 mph is dangerous enough on its own, but add in forty some other cars into the mix, and beat them to the finish line, is even more dangerous. I love danger. I am so in my element right now.

I have gone out today three times. The first and second time I have gone to the garage for adjustments. The third time my car was perfect. I am taking it out one last time before qualifying later today. I start at the line and take off when Carl says I'm clear. I push my foot to the floor and in a matter of seconds,

I'm in turn two. This car is smooth and very fast. Fuck yeah! I pass the finish line in no time at all. I go another lap and another.

Carl interrupts my enjoyment. *"That a boy, Hawk. But, can you save the speed for later. I don't need you tearing up the car before qualifying."*

"Ah, chill out, old man, I got this. This car is sweet."

I come down pit row and turn the car off. Honestly, I don't want to get out. If I had this car at Homestead last season, I probably would have won the championship. Instead, I finished third because I had a shit car. Goodbye old sponsors and hello to my new ones. New car, new owner and new sponsors, this is going to be my year. I can feel it.

I put the net down, put my shield up and give Carl the thumbs up. I look right at Ciara and wink at her. She has the same expression as other women have had when they learn I'm a Nascar driver. She had no idea what I do for a living. I get out of my car and go over the wall. I climb up the pit box and watch the video that I know Carl will have waiting for me.

I look at Ciara. *"Where is your puppy?"*

"I assume Pat took her when Bethany dropped me off."

"We gotta go. Carl, see you later."

I jump down and help Ciara down. *"Did I do something wrong?"*

"Axel has not been left alone with other dogs before."

"You weren't kidding when you said he could eat Alaska for lunch?"

"I hope I was kidding."

I take Ciara's hand and start jogging. She struggles to stay up with me. We reach my bus and I open the door and climb the steps. Ciara is hot on my heels. She burst out laughing. I don't think it's funny. I was seriously worried about her dog.

"Some beast you have there!"

Yeah, yeah. So the dogs are snuggled together on Axle's doggy bed. I'll take that over him eating hers for a snack. To get her to stop laughing, I turn and face her.

"Welcome home, Sweetheart."

"What do you mean home?"

"This is your home for the next month."

"Please tell me you are taking the fold-down table."

I laugh. I mean really laugh. *"Oh no, Sweetheart, I sleep in my bed. After last night, you'll be right next to me."*

"I'm not sleeping with you."

"I guess you get the pull-out couch since the table doesn't fold down."

"Well, aren't you just a generous host."

"I offered my bed."

"Hmm-hmm."

"I gotta take him for a walk."

"I will come with you and take Alaska."

We walk our dogs and we have many eyes on us. Everyone stares at us wondering what the hell is going on. Nobody is used to seeing me with a woman inside the track. Just to make them all the more curious, I take Ciara's hand. Fuck them, let them gossip and wonder. Frankly, it's none of their business but since I know how people talk. I might as well make it worth their while.

Ciara and I take an extra-long walk. I ask her about how she ended up being an item in her Grandmother's auction. I was quite surprised to hear her side of the story. She asked me why I put in a bid and I told her the truth, that I didn't. Now she understands my reaction better. She questioned why Carl and Bethany did it. I lied and said I didn't know. I wasn't about to tell her they have this big stunt all planned out to make me look like I can do relationships and that I am pretty much going along with it, which I'm still baffled about because I don't give two shits what the public thinks. It's no skin off my back if they think I'm a player or bad boy. Hell, I even heard once that I'm secretly gay. That's quite funny. I got a good laugh out of that rumor. If they knew just how many girls I've slept with, gay would have never left their mouths. I never responded to that rumor.

"What is Bethany's deal?"

"I'm not sure what you are asking me."

"She's kinda a bitch."

That strikes me as odd Ciara said that. *"Really? She's never come off that way to me. No one's ever said that to me before."*

"Must be it's just me she doesn't like then."

"It doesn't matter to me if she does or doesn't. I like you." She smiles. Ciara really is a beautiful woman. If I were looking to settle down she'd be the type I'd go for. She's sweet, seems to have a good head on her shoulders and it helps that she is hot as fuck. I am not looking for a wife, though, especially one that has to date, ten other men. *"What number guy am I again?"*

"You are the second one."

We stop walking. I face her. For some unknown reason, I kiss her. *"I have to tell you the truth. I am not looking for a relationship. Carl cooked up this crazy idea to use this month as a publicity stunt to help my image."*

"So, you are sleeping on the pull-out couch?"

"Doesn't being honest count for something?"

"For the next month, we pretend we are in love for the cameras? Got it!"

Ciara walks off. I knew I should not have told her. This is why I don't do relationships. They are too damn complicated. Plus they are time consuming and too much work. My first love is my car and my career. I don't have time for anything else.

"Ciara, wait."

I jog to catch up to her. *"Am I supposed to hold your hand right now?"*

"I didn't do that for the cameras. I held your hand because I wanted to."

She looks to her left and so do I. She spins around and stands in front of me. She kisses me. I bring her in closer and deepen the kiss. When she removes her lips, I want to bring them back to mine. Am I doing this for a show? That kiss sure as hell didn't feel like it.

CHAPTER NINE
CIARA

I am pissed! I walk so fast back to Hawk's bus that my puppy can't keep up. I stop and pick her up to carry her since her little legs can't go so fast. I hear Hawk call out my name. I glance back and see him jogging toward me. I keep going but I do slow my pace. I am being a bitch when I ask him if we should be holding hands. Blah, blah! I see a person stalking us with a camera in hand. I turn and kiss Hawk giving Carl what he wants. I think Carl should go fuck himself. I am not pissed off at Hawk, but his manager is another story. I am even madder at myself. I have this great guy who cares about me in California and here I am in Florida having sex with a guy who has no desire to have a girlfriend. I am a hot fucking mess. I feel like I have no idea what I am doing. Right now, I'm not so worried about my heart as I am my mind. Okay, I'm extremely worried about both.

We get back to the bus and I follow Hawk inside. I set Alaska to the floor. Axel comes over to me and smells me. I laugh. I think I just got snubbed by a dog when he doesn't let me pet him. He picks my puppy up and I almost freaked. Apparently, Axel thinks Alaska is his. He carried her over to the doggy bed and dropped her. He then snuggles up with her. I look at Hawk. I want to tell him his beast is a wimp, but I decide to keep my joke to myself.

"Are you alright? I understand if you are pissed at me."

"I am pissed, but not at you."

"What can I do to make it better?"

"I'll be fine. I just need to process everything."

"Did you have a connection with the first guy?"

"I'm not supposed to talk about the relationship with you. However, I don't care about the rules right now. So, yes we had a connection. A very good one."

"You are really going to pick one guy at the end of this and marry them?"

"I don't know. I guess we don't have to worry about you being on that list."

He looks away. *"I guess not."* He puts his hand on the counter and leans forward, getting lost in thought.

Hawk is a tall man. His hair is dark and he has a

shaggy haircut or skaters cut. Whatever it's called. His eyes are bluish-gray and dreamy. They are quite stunning. He keeps his face clean shaven. So far I would say he wears his emotions on his sleeve. If he's stressed or annoyed he comes off as grumpy. If he sees something he wants he goes for it as he did last night. When he's excited, he's playful and happy. I think we are both the same when it comes to being exposed for all to see. We can't hide the way we feel.

"Penny for your thoughts."

"Only a penny, huh?"

He picks one up off the counter. *"It's all I have on hand."*

"How long are we here? You race all over the states, right?"

"We are here for two weeks. The 500 isn't until next week. We've been off for the last two months so this week is like getting us back in the saddle."

"You have practice again today?"

"Yep. My teammates and I will get the track for an hour. After that, I am free to do whatever you want."

"I don't have anything in mind. I was just curious."

"You like seafood?"

"Some, not all."

"There's this great seafood restaurant I go to every time I'm here. I'll take you tonight." He looks at his phone when it rings. *"I have to take this."*

"Okay."

He heads outside to take the call in private. I overheard Bethany's name as he stepped off the bus. I hear him yelling at her through the open window. I heard my name. I am tempted to move over so that I can eavesdrop. A private call should be just that, private. I sit here trying my best to not hear what's going on. It's difficult when he's shouting. After a minute or two, I am getting annoyed. I mean, Christ everyone is probably listening. I can't take it. I don't need to be the center of his argument with his assistant. I get up, open the door and step outside. I tap him on the shoulder and put my hands on my hips. He looks at me. I gave him a look. He shrugs his shoulder and holds his finger up, indicating me to wait a minute. I am not waiting a minute. I grab his phone and hang it up. I march back inside the bus.

"What the hell was that?"

I close the window and check for others that may be open. *"Everyone doesn't need to hear you yelling at Bethany about me. I didn't tell you she's a bitch for you to run back and let her know I said that."*

"For one, I don't care what people think. She

treated you like shit and I'm going to let her know it is not acceptable."

"You told whoever was listening that dating me was hers and Carl's idea for your public image. Not wise if you are using me to show people we are a couple."

"Maybe I don't want to use you."

"I can go home. I could tell Grams we don't get along."

"That's not happening."

"Why not? You said it yourself, you don't do relationships."

"Because I like you." I let out a puff of air. He gets a cocky smirk on his face. *"Want to do something I am sure you've never done before?"*

"Like what?"

"It's a surprise. You just have to trust me."

"I don't know you well enough to trust you."

"You will after this. Give me a second to set it up."

"Okay."

Nothing like a conversation change during a discussion.

He types away on his phone and I'm getting nervous. I get the feeling Hawk is very spontaneous and daring. I am far from either one of those characteristics. He smiles the entire time he's communicating with whomever he's texting to. He finally sets his phone down and asks if I'm ready. Am I ready? Hell no! But do I want to trust him? Yes! So far meeting Hawk has been rocky. I am all for finding safe ground to stand on.

We get outside and I have to say I'm relieved when he tells me to get in his car. His everyday car, not his race car. Being at a race track, he could have cooked up any daring, dangerous idea in that head of his.

"Are we leaving the track?"

"Nope. I am taking you around the track. That's better than leaving."

"You're going to drive slow, right?"

He just smirks. Oh Lord, help me! I double check my seatbelt. Shouldn't I have safety gear? A helmet? Can I just get out and watch? Hawk doesn't know me well enough to know I am not daring.

"Ready?"

"Umm, okay." I close my eyes. I can feel the car moving, but it doesn't feel like we are going very fast at all. I peeked an eye open and then both of them. I look over at Hawk who has a huge grin. *"You're not going very fast."*

"Because you are scared and don't trust me."

I glance out the window and I see the empty stands. I think about if it were full of fans, how it must look to Hawk going 200mph. It's probably a blur. Like if you blink you'll miss it sort of thing. I check my seatbelt again. I grab the armrest in one hand and grab the seat with my other.

"Okay, I'm ready."

He laughs. *"You must be a riot at an amusement park."*

"Hey!"

"Hold on, Baby, I'm about to give you the ride of your life."

We did a full lap and then as promised, Hawk pushes in the clutch and shifts gears. I smile big. We are flying around the track, going so fast I'm scared to look at just how fast we are going. We do five laps before he slows the car. Then he parks back at the bus.

"What did you think?"

"That was so much fun!" I can't stop smiling. We get out of the car and we meet at the front of it and I leap into his arms. *"I want to do it again!"*

He kisses me and damn he's a great kisser. I run my fingers into his hair. I feel his hand slide lower to my ass. He presses his body closer to mine. We kiss until we hear someone whistling. When we break apart I scan the area. I don't see any cameras. Did he kiss me because he wanted to?

Hawk tells me he has to go practice. He asks if I want to sit with Carl or hang back here on his bus. I tell him I want to watch him. He smacks my ass and winks at me. He's being playful and I like it.

CHAPTER TEN
HAWK

I climb out of my car and I am stoked! This car is amazingly fast. Moving into a new car and a new owner might be the best move I've made in my career. I am feeling great. I have this wonderful girl to go celebrate with tonight. Ciara has been this pleasant surprise to add to all the good that has been added to my life recently. I am looking forward to spending the evening with her. I don't have this lavish night all planned out, but I do know that it will start with dinner.

We are getting ready for dinner. I have to say, Ciara is gorgeous no matter what she wears. The dress she put on is no different. How can a woman be cute and sexy at the same time? I cannot deny I am attracted to her. Very attracted. I am starting to like her more than I thought I would.

"You look so handsome, Mr. Evans." She straightens my suit jacket and smiles.

"You look radiant, Ms. Verbank. I am honored to have you as my date tonight."

"Really? More than for the cameras?"

I am wishing I didn't tell her why she's here. I don't want her to question if I kiss her for cameras or if I do it because that's what I want to do. *"Every time I have held your hand, kissed you or even had sex with you has never been for the cameras. I have done it because I wanted to. When I'm around you, I feel open and raw. The reason you are here was because of Carl and Bethany. The reason you are still here is because I want you here. I want to know you, Ciara. I am drawn to you and I want to see where it goes."*

"What about the part you don't want a relationship?"

"Maybe I was wrong in thinking I can't have both. Maybe I can have my career and you."

"We are going to see where this leads?"

"We have a month, right? Let's see where it takes us."

"Okay."

"Let's go and have our first date. Let's be open and raw together."

"Sounds good to me, but I have to do this." She

reaches up and takes my tie off. She unbuttons a couple of buttons. *"There, that looks more like your style."*

I can't help myself when I kiss her. I wouldn't complain if she would have kept going with my clothes. I am all for staying in and having my way with her body. However, I know I have to prove to her I do know how to be a boyfriend and that I do have a romantic side to me.

Our meal is sitting in front of us. The way she moans during eating is distracting. My manhood is fully aware of the sweet sounds she is making. Every time she moans, I know those are the same moans she makes during sexual pleasure. I am not ashamed to admit she is turning me on. So much so that I'm tempted to drag her out of here and find a private spot and make her moan for me. I am fighting that urge as I am trying to be a good boy and show her I can do this whole relationship thing.

"That was crazy to watch you race around that track with your teammates. Don't you ever get scared?"

"I've lived and breathed racing since I was a kid.

Every time I get into a car, I feel this rush that I can't explain or put into words how much I am made for racing." She licks the butter off her fingers after dipping her crab leg. She really needs to stop making love to her food. It's literally driving me crazy. *"Tell me about you. Has fashion always been your passion?"*

She tells me all about herself. She lights up when she talks about her designs. I see a different side of her and I like it. She is very humble and doesn't seek attention when really she probably deserves it. When I say humble, the way she talks she acts as if it weren't for her grandmother she probably would not be so successful. I doubt that's true. You can't have a career or hobby that you're so passionate about and not be successful. People like us thrive on it. Nothing matters but living and breathing our dreams.

"Are you ready to get out of here? I have a place I'd like to take you for dessert."

"Really? Where?"

"It's a surprise."

"Let's do it."

I pay the bill and we get the hell out of here. We don't take my car. We walk instead. I take her hand when we start walking, our fingers lace together and I feel this bond beginning to grow. I was blindsided by this girl's entrance in my life. I am ready to give this a real chance of building a relationship with my eyes wide open. Where I want to take her isn't that far. I'm ready to see her in her element. Besides, what woman out there doesn't like shopping on the strip?

We approach the strip and Ciara sees all the shops that line the beachfront. Her eyes light up. I was right to bring her here. Shopping is only one reason I brought her. I am ready to see the carefree side of her to come out again. I get a feeling she has a hard time letting loose and be a little wild.

"Oh, Hawk this has you written all over it." She puts this thin strip of material around my neck.

"A scarf, really?"

"Heck yes. Next time you have an event, you could forget the tie and add a scarf for an accessory instead. It's got that cocky, cool vibe. A tie is too uptight for you."

"Is that a bad thing, that ties aren't me?"

"No, the way people dress should match their personality. It's okay to be different and also be comfortable."

"We will take it," I tell the shop owner.

We continue to shop at many other places. I have

a hand full of bags that are filled with new stuff for me. Ciara had a field day picking out new clothes for me. I wanted to spoil her. That didn't happen, but she's happy and that makes me happy.

We stop at one last place. She picks up a bracelet. She smiles and grabs my wrist. *"I'm supposed to be spoiling you."*

She picks up another one. *"We'll get matching ones."*

I put it on her wrist. She kisses my cheek. We see a flash and we both look. I open my wallet and throw a hundred bucks at the lady working. I take Ciara's hand. *"Ready to make a run for it?"*

Ciara laughs as we start running toward the pier. We look over our shoulders to see if we were followed. When we stop running we both just look at each other and laugh all over again. I bring her to me and hug her. I really really like this woman. Oddly, I'm not even worried she won't fit into my plans for my future. I think she's perfect for me. I believe Ciara can be the one to break me of the bad boy image I have going on.

"I once was in love with this girl I dated for three years."

"What happened to her?"

"She didn't want to be a racer's wife. She said she couldn't handle knowing I could wreck and possibly die. I didn't understand it since she met me at a track. She knew who I was when she met me. I think what she couldn't handle was the spotlight that comes with being a professional driver. She hated women wanting a picture with me or an autograph. Some women get a little too touchy and inappropriate."

"How long has it been?"

"Almost three years. In those three years, I haven't dated. It's why everyone thinks I'm this player that only sleeps with women for sex. What they don't realize is that I had my heartbroken. I don't want that to happen again." Ciara pushes out of my arms and steps away. I feel like she's ready to run. I grab her hand and she yanks it away. *"Talk to me. Don't shut me out."*

"Hawk, I can't let you be open, raw, exposed, or whatever you want to call it with me."

"Why the hell not? We have something beautiful starting here. I know you feel it too."

"I do feel it. In the two days we've known each other it feels like we've already hit speed bumps and went over them like they were not going to stop this connection we have."

"Exactly, so why the sudden step backward?"

"Because what if you fall in love with me and in the end I'm that girl who isn't going to be your wife? I don't want to be the reason you put walls back up if we don't work out."

I take her face in my hands and force her to look at me. *"I don't know if this is going to turn into love for either one of us, but I sure do want to find out. I'm willing to take a chance of finding love with you. If I end up broken-hearted in the end, then at least I will know I gave love a chance. It's no different than you taking this chance with every guy you have to date."*

"I don't know."

"There's no reverse here. We gotta stop hitting these speedbumps and plow right over them as if they aren't there. Do this with me." She tries to look away. *"Take the leap with me. No more going backward."*

"Take the leap," she whispered. I kiss her. I give her a reason to give me a chance. Give us a chance. *"No more going backward."*

"Yep! Only forward."

Another flash. She takes my hand and we run. We stop at the end of the pier. There's nowhere else to run. Ciara pulls me toward the Ferris wheel. She butted in line. She tells the young man attending the ride who I am. He lets us on. Ciara sits close to me, I put an arm around her and she rests her head on me. We reach the top and she leans forward and waves to the crowd. When she sits back her lips are on mine as the ride moves again. We kiss and kiss some more. I think it's time we get out of the public eye. I am definitely ready to share my bed with my girlfriend.

CHAPTER ELEVEN
CIARA

Hawk called Pat to come and pick us up before we got off the ferris wheel. Neither one of us wanted to deal with the guy following us around to take more pictures of us. We stayed on the ride longer than we were supposed to just so that we didn't have to deal with it. When Pat let Hawk know she was here, we got off and took off running toward the car. She is going to drop us off at his car that we left at the restaurant. Hawk brings out a side of me that's new. A side of me that I want to explore more. My Grams put me in a position to be adventurous and have fun. Why not take this opportunity and go with it. No harm in having fun. There's no harm in being a little more wild.

Pat pulls up behind Hawk's car. We get out and he walks me to the passenger side. He uses the remote to unlock the car. When he reaches for the handle, I touch his arm.

"I'm not ready to go back."

"Really? What do you have in mind?" I nod my head toward the ocean. *"You want to go swimming?"*

"Swimming or other things."

"Ms. Verbank, are you suggesting we get down and dirty in the sand?"

"Maybe."

"You do know that's a public beachfront right?"

"It's dark enough out, right?" I begin to walk away. *"I'm going swimming with or without you, Mr. Evans."*

"You realize it's February!"

I keep walking. *"You do realize I really don't care about swimming, right?"*

I smile when I hear the sound of his car when he locks the doors. I slow my pace to wait for him to catch up to me. His hand goes to my waist when he comes up behind me. His mouth is near my ear when he tells me he'll race me to the water. His hand falls away and without warning, he takes off jogging toward the ocean. I take my sandals off and drop them, then I take off running. His laugh echoes in the night. My feet hit the cold water and I jumped back. Damn, it's much colder than I thought it would be. Hawk takes my hands and he tells me to go for a walk with him. I walk with him on my right and to my left, the ocean crashes against my feet. I move over closer to him and lean my head on his arm as we walk. We reach an old wooden dock and go under it instead of walking around it. Hawk swings around in front of me and kisses me. Out of nowhere the wind picked up and raindrops drip through the cracks, hitting us. Hawk starts to move and I step back as he steps forward. I gasp as my back makes contact with a beam. Hawk presses his body into mine. He deepens the kiss. A hand cups my breast as he kisses me with such control and dominance. I grab unto his ass, wanting him closer.

"Do you trust me yet?"

I answer with bated breath. *"Yes."*

Hawk takes a few steps away. My hands fall to my sides. He takes the scarf off that I picked out for him tonight. He smirks. He told me to hold out my wrists and I do. He loops the scarf around my wrists, binding them together. He ties a knot and tells me to test its hold. I try to separate my wrists by twisting and pulling.

"Put your hands above your head."

I do as I'm told. Hawk walks around behind me, taking the loose ends of the scarf, he ties my wrists to the beam. He comes back around to stand in front of me. His eyes travel the length of my body. He then steps forward. His hands grab my bound wrists as he kisses me. He bites my lower lip before he steps back again, running his fingertips down my arms. I shake my head as the rain picks up and begins to soak my hair, my clothes, and my skin. I can feel my nipples harden. My pussy is wet. I am so damn turned on.

Hawk reaches out and his thumb moves over my nipple. I squeeze my legs together. I gasp when suddenly he rips my dress open. I am sure I have no buttons left on the sundress. I don't really care about that right now. My breasts are freed from my bra when he undoes the front clasp. I swallow when the cold rain drips down on my nipples. Hawk slides my panties past my hips, down my thighs and my calves. He lifts one foot at a time and discards them fully. His fingers trace up my legs and I squeeze my thighs together. He spreads my legs apart and I moan when he touches my pussy. I moan again when he enters me. His mouth kisses my lower stomach, all the way up my torso to my chest. He sucks one of my breasts into his mouth. I wish my hands were free. I want to touch him. Dig my fingernails into his skin. I want him so close that I breathe in his scent. This unpredictable man is getting to me. I want his manhood inside me and to leap into an orgasmic bliss together.

"Fuck me, Hawk," I say with desperation in my voice.

His hands fall from my body. His lips move off my flesh. He stares into my eyes. I want to reach out and rip his clothes off. I cannot do anything but wait.

"Ciara, do you have any idea how sexy you are right now?"

"No."

"You're stunningly sexy." He reaches into his pocket and gets out his phone. What the hell is he doing? I try to pull my arms free. It's no use. He holds the phone up. I turn my head away. He takes a picture of me bound and tied to a beam. My wet body is exposed as my wet dress hangs open at my sides. Why would he do this to me? *"Look at me."*

"No! Untie me!"

"That picture isn't for me. It's for you."

"What do you mean for me?"

"So that you can see what I see when I look at you."

Hawk kisses me. He opens his pants as his tongue takes over my mouth. He then lifts me off my feet and puts my legs around him. He holds my weight up with one hand and uses his other to guide his cock inside me. He lowers my body.

"Fuck!" I say when he's fully inside me.

The scarf around my wrists gets tighter as he thrusts in and out of me. The waves crashing into the shore drown out my moans. He feels amazing fucking my pussy. This sex is risky, hot and raw desire. He has managed to make me live dangerously and I love every second of it. I want more. More of him and more of this wilder side of me.

Hawk groans in my ear. My arms fall. Pain shoots through them as blood rushes to my hands. Hawk lowers me to the ground. He slams his cock back inside me. My pussy strokes his manhood as he takes me faster. He groans again and thrust inside me hard. I let go. I orgasm as his movements stop. His breathing is heavy. I can feel his chest pounding as his weight lowers on top of me. When he rolls off of me the rain pours down on our bodies. I blink my eyes a few times. Out of nowhere, I smile. I look at Hawk and he's staring right at me.

"You make me feel something I've never felt before."

"What is that?"

"Freedom."

"I should probably get you out of this rain."

"I can't wait to see what another day is going to be like with you." I bite my lower lip. *"But tomorrow isn't here yet."*

I get up and straddle his body. His cock is still hard, so I lower myself onto him. Once, twice, I might as well get the third time out of the way right now.

CHAPTER TWELVE
CIARA

For the last week, Hawk and I haven't left the bus very much. It's been difficult to keep our hands off one another. The sex is unbelievably good. But there is more to us than just the sex. Hawk is better at relationships than he thinks he is. He has cooked me dinners, we've watched romantic movies, and we have stayed up all hours of the night talking with him telling me stories of himself growing up. I know things such as, he has two sisters and he's the oldest. I know that his parents have been married for thirty years. He started racing after his father took him to the local races for a father-son night out. I also know that he does not own a home even though he could own a few. Someday when he gets married, he wants to get married in the same church as his parents got married in. Hawk's laughter, wild side, and spontaneous nature are contagious. He brings out things in me that I never even knew were inside. It's one of the qualities I like about him.

It's Hawk's big week. He said this race is the super bowl of racing. Every driver, crew chief, and team want to win this race. It's more than a race. Winning the 500 is a prestigious honor. He really wants this win. He knows he has the car to do it.

Hawk comes over to where I am chilling on the couch. He tells me he has to do some stuff before the race. He gives me a kiss before he leaves. Axel and Alaska stand at the door, waiting for him to come back. After time passes Axel lays down and has a sad look on his face. It makes me wonder if Alaska gets sappy when I leave. Then I start thinking about Malcolm. I miss him. It's confusing to miss one guy, but also share a connection with another one. Malcolm and Hawk are different in many ways. I know if I'm with Malcolm he's romantic. What woman doesn't like romance? If I end up with Hawk my life would be unpredictable but exciting.

I bend over and pick up my puppy. *"How in the world am I going to pick the right person for me, Alaska? Your daddy got me you so that I don't forget him. Here I am sharing you with another man. Don't worry, I'm not forgetting him."*

Alaska curls up on my lap. She puts her head

down and looks in the opposite direction then looks at me.

I lean my head back and stare at the ceiling. I feel horrible that this is Hawk's big day and I want to hear Malcolm's voice. I want to know he is handling me being with another man. Hell, I want to know if he misses me. If he's thinking about me. This isn't fucking fair. Why can't I talk to him? Why did Grams make that stupid rule? I should be able to talk to Malcolm. I should be able to talk to Hawk next month when I'm with someone else if I want. Why can't I make some of my own rules? It is my life after all.

I reach for my phone. I swipe the screen and bring up my contacts. I scroll through all the names and find Malcolm's number. I tap on call. I put the phone up to my ear. It rings once, twice, and I hear his voice say my name. I panic and hang up. My heart is beating so damn fast. My phone rings and I almost drop it. I stare at the screen wanting desperately to answer it, but I don't. Axel picks his head up and looks at me. It's like he knows I did something bad. My hands are shaky. I feel sick to my stomach. My phone goes silent. I set it on the couch next to me. I throw my head back and run my hands down my face. I pick my phone back up when my text message sound goes off. I open the message.

Malcolm: Tell me you are okay!

Me: I am. I'm just thinking about you.

Me: Are you okay?

Malcolm: I'm getting by.

Me: I have to go. I just wanted to hear your voice.

I put my phone down as if it's burning my fingers. Fuck, I shouldn't have done that. The bus door whips open. *"Hey, I wanna show you something."*

"Okay."

I get my shoes on. I am feeling awfully guilty right now. I bite my bottom lip when my phone chimes again. I swipe it off the couch and read the message.

Malcolm: I know that feeling. I miss you. I think about you non-stop. This is fucking hard, Ciara. I am holding onto hope with a death grip.

"Ready?" Hawk asks.

I smile a fake smile. *"Yep."* We get in a golf cart once we are outside. *"Where are we going?"*

"To meet some of my fans."

I really feel like I am going to get sick. I sure picked bad timing with getting in touch with Malcolm. God, I'm such an idiot. Sometimes I wonder if my bad choice of men in the past has to do with self-destruction. I sure do know how to make a mess in the relationship department. No wonder why I was in a bad relationship with Hunter. I mess everything up when it's good.

I take a deep breath, trying to compose myself to meet Hawk's fans. He asks if I'm nervous and I play off his thoughts. He has no idea what I just did. A part of me wants to blurt it out. A bigger part of me says no fucking way. He doesn't need to know his girlfriend contacted her other boyfriend on the biggest day of racing. My Grams did this to find me a man worthy enough to be with me. It's probably more like if I'm worthy enough to be with them.

CHAPTER THIRTEEN
CIARA

The last two weeks have flown by. Being with Hawk has been an experience I'll never forget. Being part of his life this past month, I got to know a side of him he hides from the public. Hell, I think he hides it from himself. He has a big heart. He's kind, caring, and he does have a romantic side to him. It just took him time to show me. Hawk is a man that I could see myself with long-term. But I also say that about Malcolm. It's been difficult, it's been a test of the type of person I really am. I have a feeling it's going to continue being a test for the next eight months. I still haven't figured out how I can separate these men from one another. I've met two amazing guys. They have different qualities and different lifestyles. But in the end, I could see myself marrying either one of them. I have eight more men that I have to date and I have no idea how I'm going to keep a clear head and an open heart. Because right now my heart is pretty damn full.

Hawk and I are on his private plane. He was supposed to put me in a car and have Pat drive me to the airport. We were supposed to say goodbye a couple of hours ago. He told me he wasn't ready to say goodbye just yet. I sort of wished he would've done what he was supposed to do. I am not good at goodbyes. I think it would've been easier to walk away from him if I had Pat drive me to the airport. Rip that band-aid off and get it over with. Instead, I have him flying me home. I have to walk off this plane when we land and know he's taking off as soon as I do. We already broke Grams rules by me staying a couple of extra days. When I step off this plane, I am walking right into another man's life. I don't get those three or four days at home to collect myself. I probably shouldn't have stayed longer. But Hawk is so spontaneous I went along with it because he brings that out in me.

I look over at Hawk lost in thought. I want to ask what he is thinking about. I can probably guess what he's thinking about, I am thinking that too. Why do we have to separate? What we have is good. People don't break up when things are good. They stay together forever or at least until things fall apart. We aren't falling apart. We are a solid couple just as Malcolm and I were. Ugh! I hate this.

"Ciara, I want you to know something."

"Okay."

"First, what I'm about to say, you don't need to reply to or do anything at all. What I want to tell you isn't for a response. It's so that you know where I stand."

"Okay." I have butterflies in my belly. He hasn't said he loves me and if he says he does, I don't know that I can walk away from him.

"This past month with you has been thrilling. I have enjoyed every second that we have been together. From the moment I found out that you were in that go-kart, I had this connection to you or better yet, this amazing attraction to you. We sure had a bumpy start to our relationship, but what we ended up with was something incredible. You opened my eyes to something that I didn't know was lacking in my life. It's been simply amazing to have you be with me in the winner's circle, to have you next to me in the mornings, to have your hand in mine as we walked the dogs. Everything we did together I don't want it to end. I want to be with you and grow this spontaneous and raw relationship. I know the rules and I know I

GRANDMA'S SILENT AUCTION

didn't sign up for this, but I don't want it to end. You mean the world to me, Ciara."

"This isn't easy for me. I don't want what we have to end, either. I keep questioning why my relationship with Malcolm had to end. And now, I am questioning why it has to end with you. I wonder if I'll be questioning myself with everyone that I have to date. I am questioning myself if I went along with this grand plan of my Grams because I don't know who I am. Maybe in my subconscious mind, I'm in search of who I am and not the type man I need in my life. That might not make sense to you because honestly, it doesn't make sense to me either. I am an independent woman. I have gone my entire life wondering what type of person I want to give myself to. I couldn't sleep last night because I'm terrified once I walk away from you, I walk away from what I've been searching for all these years. Then, I wonder if I already walked away from the man I want. I know I shouldn't be talking about Malcolm and how I felt for him. I'm telling you because I feel the same way about you. I shouldn't be falling in love with you when I already fell in love with him. This entire situation is so fucking confusing." I cannot stop the tears from falling. "What if I didn't know that I was lacking love in my life and now I am trying to grab it and hold on *to it because I get a glimpse of it. What if I'm too fucked up, too careless with my heart and who I want in the end decides he doesn't love me? What if I put myself out there for love and in the end, nobody is there wanting to marry me? What if I want to marry you? There's no guarantee you'll still be here."* I feel like I can't breathe. I feel like I'm on the verge of having a mental breakdown.

"That's a lot of questions. I don't have all the answers for you."

The pilot's voice comes over the speaker system interrupting us to let us know that we need to get our seatbelts on because we are preparing for landing. We get our belts on and he doesn't say anything else. He just holds my hand.

Nothing has been said. The loudest sound in the world is silence. It's deafening right now. It isn't until we are on the ground that he says another word.

"Ciara Verbank, I don't think you know how incredible you truly are, how strong you are and how beautiful your soul is. I do. I see you. You are intelligent and not fucked up at all. I may not like knowing you are getting off this plane and walking into another man's arms, but I do know that what we shared is real. You need to find the person who will be your best friend, your lover and everything in

between. If you find out more about yourself in this fucked up journey, that's just an extra bonus. I wasn't going to tell you I love you, because I wanted to wait until I knew if I was your best friend, your lover and everything in between. Eight months is a hell of a long time to wait. I love you, Ciara Verbank. In eight months from now, I will put a ring on your finger if you love me in return." Hawk kisses my forehead, then my lips. He wipes my tears away. *"I love you. I'll be waiting for you to come back."*

"I love you, too, Hawk Evans."

"I know you do. I'm going into the sleeping cabin. You have to go now."

He gets to his feet, bends over and gives me one last kiss. I close my eyes and teardrops stream down my cheeks. I stand and straighten my dress. I let out a deep, deep breath. I exit his plane and head toward the airport. I need to find the restroom before I look for Barbara Melton.

About the Author

Thank you so much for taking the time to read Grandma's Silent Auction February. Word-of-mouth is crucial for any author to succeed. If you enjoyed the book, please leave a review on Amazon. Even if it's just a sentence or two. It would make all the difference and would be very much appreciated. – OXOX Michael James

Website: http://michaeljames-author332.bravesites.com/

Also by MICHAEL JAMES

If you enjoyed Grandma's Silent Auction February, you may also like my other books:

The Way We Love series:

Pink Skies At Night

Shadows At Night

Nights Are Unlimited

Concealed By The Night

Shattered At Night

Freed At Night

Winning A Cowgirl's Heart - Trilogy:

The Rodeo King

The Best Friend

The Fate Of My Heart

Winning a Cowgirl's Heart -Complete Box Set

Construction Vs. Corporate- Trilogy:

Unbalanced

Balancing

Balanced

Secrets Within a Club

Club Comrade

Revenge

Saving Club Conrad

Masquerade Saga

His Pearls

His Secrets

His Prison

His Games

His Moves

All His

Crime in Landkaster series

The Mirror

Times Like These

Grandma's Silent Auction series

January

Standalone:

Toying With October

Pieces Of Me

A Christmas For Eve

Dom Diaries: Tangled Up In You

Christmas Scavenger Hunt

Blue Christmas

Stealing the Christmas Spotlight

Co-written with Jodi Fahey

Last Sheet

Manufactured by Amazon.ca
Bolton, ON